# DALE
## EARNHARDT JR.

by Connie Colwell Miller

NASCAR
HEROES

Published by ABDO Publishing Company, PO Box 398166, Minneapolis, MN 55439. Copyright © 2013 by Abdo Consulting Group, Inc. International copyrights reserved in all countries. No part of this book may be reproduced in any form without written permission from the publisher. SportsZone™ is a trademark and logo of ABDO Publishing Company.

Printed in the United States of America,
North Mankato, Minnesota
102012
012013

Editor: Chrös McDougall
Series Designer: Becky Daum

Photo Credits: Phelan M. Ebenhack/AP Images, cover, title; Autostock, Nigel Kinrade/AP Images, cover; Scott A. Miller/AP Images, 4-5, 8-9; Russell Williams/AP Images, 5; Glenn Smith/AP Images, 6; John Raoux/AP Images, 7, 31; Don O'Reilly/ Dozier Mobley/Getty Images, 10-11; Daytona Beach News-Journal/Kelly Jordan/ AP Images, 12-13; Rusty Burroughs/AP Images, 14, 30 (top); Steve Helber/AP Images, 15; Alan Marler/AP Images, 16-17; Chuck Burton/AP Images, 18-19; Bob Rosato/Sports Illustrated/Getty Images, 20-21; David Graham/AP Images, 22, 30 (bottom); Paul Sancya/AP Images, 23, 30 (center); Matt Slocum/AP Images, 24-25; Matthew T. Thacker/AP Images, 26-27; Chris Graythen/Getty Images, 28-29

**Cataloging-in-Publication Data**
Colwell Miller, Connie.
 Dale Earnhardt, Jr. / Connie Colwell Miller.
   p. cm. -- (NASCAR heroes)
Includes bibliographical references and index.
ISBN 978-1-61783-661-9
1. Earnhardt, Dale, Jr.--Juvenile literature.  2. Automobile racing drivers--United States--Biography--Juvenile literature.  I. Title.
796.72092--dc21

[B]

2012946251

# CONTENTS

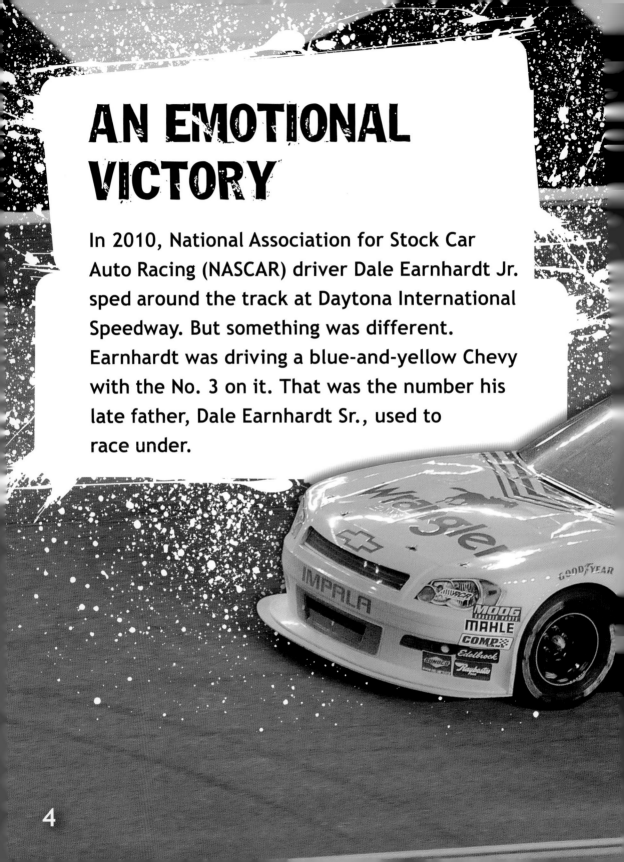

# AN EMOTIONAL VICTORY

In 2010, National Association for Stock Car Auto Racing (NASCAR) driver Dale Earnhardt Jr. sped around the track at Daytona International Speedway. But something was different. Earnhardt was driving a blue-and-yellow Chevy with the No. 3 on it. That was the number his late father, Dale Earnhardt Sr., used to race under.

Dale Earnhardt Sr.

Dale Earnhardt Jr. cruises to victory at Daytona International Speedway in 2010.

With skill and speed, Earnhardt Jr. zoomed to victory that day. It was his sixth victory in NASCAR's second-level series on that track.

Through 2011, the Earnhardt family had won 47 total races at the Daytona International Speedway.

*Earnhardt Jr. celebrates after winning the 2010 race at Daytona International Speedway in the No. 3 car.*

7

The No. 3 car Dale Earnhardt Jr. drove to victory at Daytona in 2010 was later on display at the NASCAR Hall of Fame.

*Fans were emotional when Earnhardt Jr. drove under his father's No. 3 in 2010 at Daytona.*

Earnhardt Jr.'s win at Daytona was an emotional one. It took place on the very track where his father had died nine years earlier. Fans cheered and even cried. Earnhardt Jr. had driven the No. 3 Chevy to honor his dad.

# RACING IN THE FAMILY

Ralph Dale Earnhardt Jr. was born into a racing family. His grandfather, Ralph Earnhardt, was a race car driver. His father, Dale Earnhardt Sr., is considered one of the best NASCAR drivers of all time. Earnhardt Sr. won an amazing seven NASCAR championships.

*Ralph Earnhardt began the tradition of great race car drivers in his family.*

In 2000, Dale Earnhardt Jr.
raced against his father and his
half brother in a top-level NASCAR
race. It was only the second time in
history a father had raced
with his two sons.

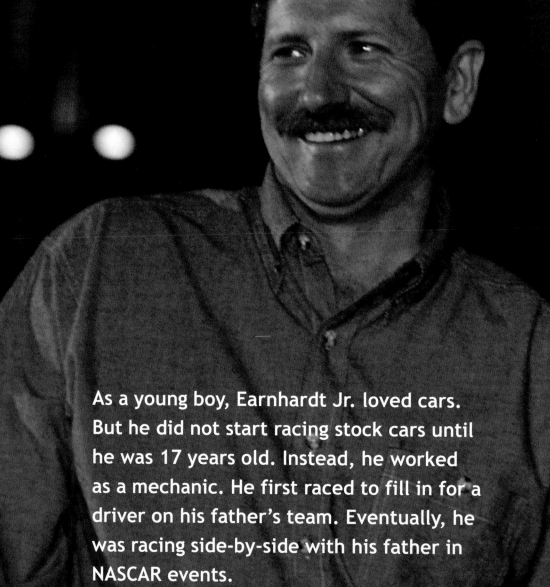

*Dale Earnhardt Sr., left, and*
*Dale Earnhardt Jr., right,*
*pose with NASCAR president*
*Bill France Jr. in 1999.*

As a young boy, Earnhardt Jr. loved cars.
But he did not start racing stock cars until
he was 17 years old. Instead, he worked
as a mechanic. He first raced to fill in for a
driver on his father's team. Eventually, he
was racing side-by-side with his father in
NASCAR events.

In 2012, Dale Earnhardt Jr. said that if he were not a race car driver, he would still be an auto mechanic.

# BIG WINS FOR JUNIOR

In 1998 and 1999, Dale Earnhardt Jr. raced full-time in NASCAR's second-level series. He won the championship both years. In 1999, he had a whopping 22 top-10 finishes. Clearly, he was ready for the big time.

*Earnhardt Jr. celebrates winning a second-level race in 1999 in Richmond, Virginia.*

15

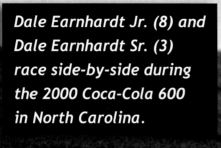

*Dale Earnhardt Jr. (8) and Dale Earnhardt Sr. (3) race side-by-side during the 2000 Coca-Cola 600 in North Carolina.*

In 2000, Earnhardt moved up to NASCAR's Cup Series. He won two races that year and finished in sixteenth place. He also became the first rookie to win NASCAR's yearly all-star race.

*Fans placed tributes in front of Dale Earnhardt Inc. headquarters in 2001 in memory of the fallen driver.*

# TRAGEDY STRIKES

In February 2001, Dale Earnhardt Jr. started the new season with excitement. The Daytona 500 starts a new NASCAR season. Earnhardt Jr. and his father started the race with their sights on the checkered flag. On the last lap, Dale Earnhardt Sr. crashed. Dale Jr. finished second. Sadly, his father died.

NASCAR fans were devastated. Earnhardt Sr. had been very popular. Earnhardt Jr. struggled with the loss, too. For a few months after his father died, Earnhardt Jr. performed poorly on the track. He was numb with grief. But he returned to Daytona for a different race in July. Amazingly, Earnhardt Jr. won the race!

Earnhardt Jr. crosses the finish line first at the 2001 Pepsi 400 just months after his father died on the same track.

Dale Earnhardt Sr.
and Dale Earnhardt
Jr. are one of only
three father and
son pairs to win the
Daytona 500 through
2012. Earnhardt Jr.
won in 2004.

*Earnhardt Jr. cruises during a 2003 race at Daytona International Speedway.*

# JUNIOR STAYS STRONG

Over the next two years, Dale Earnhardt Jr. raced better than ever. In fact, 2003 was the best year of his career yet. He finished third in NASCAR's Cup Series. He was also voted NASCAR's most popular driver.

*Earnhardt Jr. jokes with Tony Stewart in 2003. They are two of NASCAR's most popular drivers.*

*Earnhardt Jr. at a 2010 race in Pennsylvania.*

In 2004 and 2006, Earnhardt Jr. finished fifth in the Sprint Cup Series championship. He qualified for the Chase in 2004, 2006, 2008, 2011, and 2012. He also won NASCAR's Most Popular Driver Award nine times in a row.

# MORE TO COME

Dale Earnhardt Jr. still races in the Sprint Cup Series. With 18 total victories to his name through 2011, he has already had a successful career.

The pit crew works on Earnhardt Jr.'s car during a 2012 race in New Hampshire.

## FAST FACT

Dale Earnhardt Jr.
is the owner of a
NASCAR team called
JR Motorsports.

Even without a Sprint Cup title, Earnhardt Jr. is a fan favorite. NASCAR lovers everywhere like his down-to-earth personality and winning charm. Fans know one thing for sure: NASCAR is more interesting because of Junior.

*Earnhardt Jr. has long been a NASCAR fan favorite.*

# TIMELINE

**1974**

Ralph Dale Earnhardt Jr. is born on October 10 in Kannapolis, North Carolina.

**1998**

Earnhardt Jr. wins the NASCAR second-level series championship.

**1999**

Earnhardt Jr. wins the NASCAR second-level series championship again.

**2000**

Earnhardt Jr. races his rookie year in the NASCAR Cup Series. He races against his father and half-brother.

**2001**

Dale Earnhardt Sr. dies in a collision at Daytona International Speedway on February 18. Dale Earnhardt Jr. finishes second in the race.

**2003**

Earnhardt Jr. comes in third place in the NASCAR Sprint Cup championship.

**2004**

Earnhardt Jr. wins the Daytona 500.

**2010**

Earnhardt Jr. wins a second-level race at Daytona International Speedway in July. He races with his father's car and number.

# GLOSSARY

## Chase
The last 10 races of the NASCAR Cup Series. Only the top 10 drivers and two wild cards qualify to race in the Chase.

## Cup Series
NASCAR's top series for professional stock car drivers. It has been called the Sprint Cup Series since 2008.

## Daytona 500
The most famous stock car race in the world and one of the races in the Sprint Cup Series.

## owner
The person who owns an entire racing team. This person hires everyone on the team, including the driver and the crew.

## rookie
A driver in his or her first full-time season in a new series.

## second-level series
NASCAR's second-level series for professional stock car drivers. It has been called the Nationwide Series since 2008.

## series
A racing season that consists of several races.

## stock car
Race cars that resemble models of cars that people drive every day.

# INDEX